Springtime in BUGLAND!

by David A. Carter

Ready-to-Read

Simon Spotlight

New York   London   Toronto   Sydney   New Delhi

SIMON SPOTLIGHT

An imprint of Simon & Schuster Children's Publishing Division

1230 Avenue of the Americas, New York, New York 10020

SIMON SPOTLIGHT, READY-TO-READ, and colophon are registered trademarks of Simon & Schuster, Inc.

For information about special discounts for bulk purchases,

please contact Simon & Schuster Special Sales at 1-866-506-1949 or business@simonandschuster.com.

Manufactured in the United States of America 0212 LAK

First Edition

2 4 6 8 10 9 7 5 3 1

Library of Congress Cataloging-in-Publication Data

Carter, David A.

Springtime in Bugland! / by David A. Carter. — 1st ed.

p. cm. — (Ready-to-read)

Summary: When spring comes to Bugland, all the bugs celebrate.

ISBN 978-1-4424-3890-3 (pbk.)

ISBN 978-1-4424-3892-7 (hardcover)

ISBN 978-1-4424-3893-4 (eBook)

[etc.]

[1. Stories in rhyme. 2. Insects—Fiction. 3. Spring—Fiction.] I. Title.

PZ8.3.C244Sp 2012

[E]—dc23   2011027067

Spring has come
to Bugland!

The Bugs all shout
and cheer,
"Hippity, hip, hooray!"

They decide to throw a party for this very special day!

The Sunshine Bug is shining with a twinkle in his eye.

The Spelling Bees are buzzing under big blue skies.

Now that spring has come at last, the Blooming Bug can hardly wait.

There is just so much
to see and do.
It is time to celebrate!

Of all the Bugs
in Bugland,
Busy Bug loves spring
most of all.

Busy loves spring
much more than
summer, winter
or fall.

Busy Bug rides his skateboard quickly down the street.

At the pumpkin house,
Busy has a very
important Bug to meet.

"Come outside, Bitsy Bee!" shouts Busy Bug. "Spring has come to town!"

Busy looks for Bitsy everywhere, but she is not around.

Busy Bug rolls past the
pet store.
He rides around the
giant peach.

Busy feels worried.
"Where could tiny
Bitsy Bee be?"

Busy zooms past the library, but Bitsy Bee is still not there.

Busy Bug starts to
wonder if little Bitsy
is anywhere!

From around the corner of City Hall, Busy Bug hears a small giggle.

Then he sees a green bush begin to shake and wiggle!

"Buzz. Buzz. I got you, Busy Bug!" says Bitsy Bee. "Now, let's have some fun!"

"All the Bugs are ready
to play now that spring
has begun!"

Hooray for spring in
Bugland!